For my granddaughter, the amazing
Lee Van Meer Grainger — L.B.

To Landon — J.A.

Text copyright © 2020 by Linda Bailey
Illustrations © 2020 by Joy Ang

Tundra Books, an imprint of Penguin Random House Canada Young Readers,
a Penguin Random House Company

Library and Archives Canada Cataloguing in Publication

Title: Princesses versus dinosaurs / Linda Baily ; [illustrated by] Joy Ang.
Names: Bailey, Linda, 1948- author. | Ang, Joy, illustrator.
Identifiers: Canadiana (print) 20190159928 | Canadiana (ebook) 20190159944 |
ISBN 9780735264298 (hardcover) | ISBN 9780735264304 (EPUB)
Classification: LCC PS8553.A3644 P75 2020 | DDC jC813/.54—dc23

Published simultaneously in the United States of America by Tundra Books of
Northern New York, an imprint of Penguin Random House Canada Young Readers,
a Penguin Random House Company

Library of Congress Control Number: 2019947072

Edited by Tara Walker with assistance from Margot Blankier
Designed by John Martz
The artwork in this book was created digitally.
The text was set in Deccan Medium, CCGeekSpeakTweak and
CCBryanTalbotLower.

Printed and bound in China

www.penguinrandomhouse.ca

1  2  3  4  5      24  23  22  21  20

Penguin
Random House
tundra | TUNDRA BOOKS

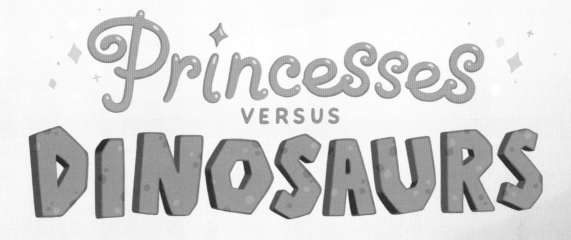

# Princesses VERSUS DINOSAURS

WRITTEN BY

## Linda Bailey

ILLUSTRATED BY

## Joy Ang

tundra

*This* is a princess book. Tra la! Tra la! Tra la!

It's all about princesses wearing sparkly tiaras and lovely silk dresses and little glass slippers and —

NO! It's not! Wrong, wrong, wrong!

This is a *dinosaur* book. It's a roaring, stomping, bone-crushing, earth-shaking *dinosaur* book!

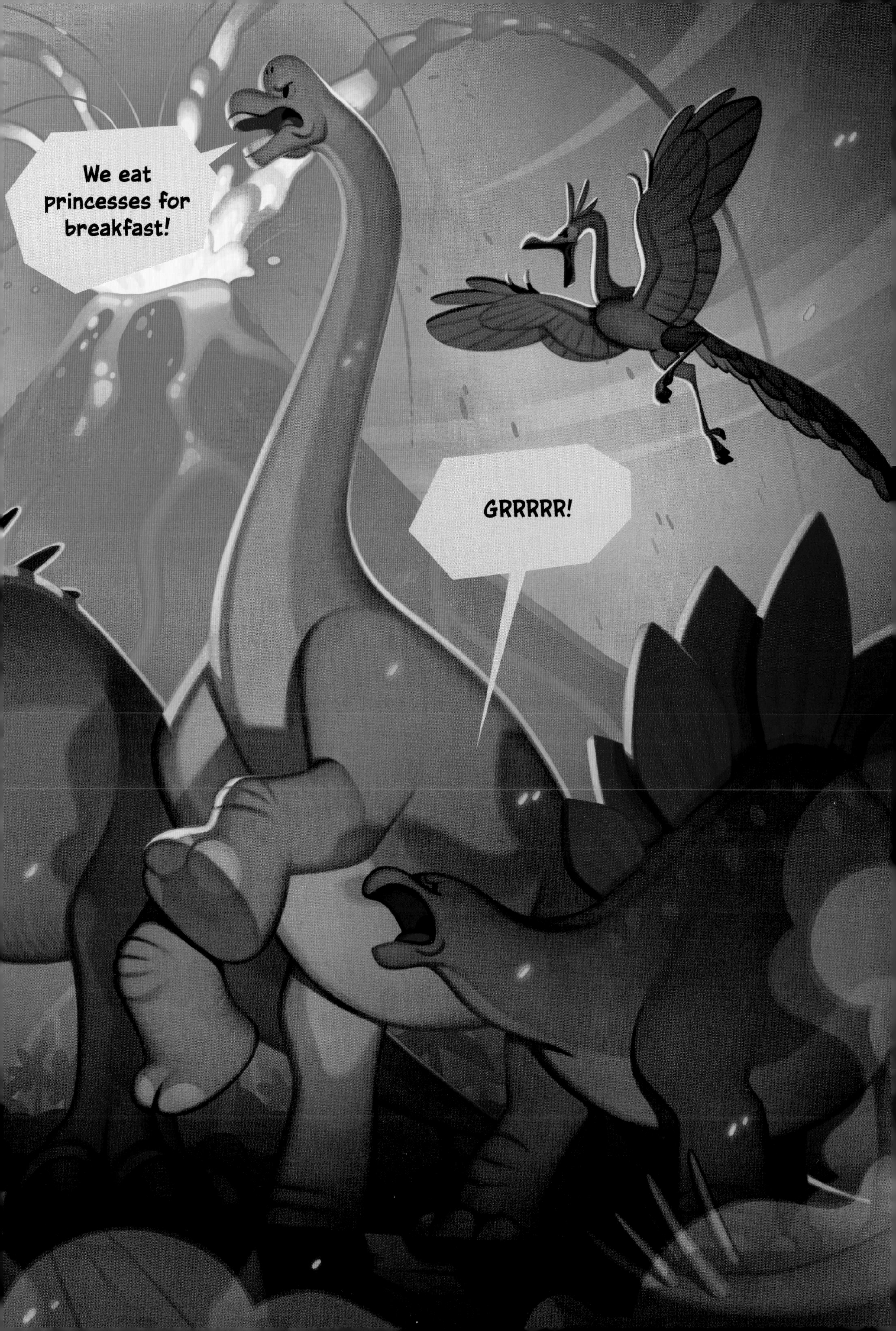
We eat princesses for breakfast!
GRRRRR!

Uh-oh. We seem to have
a mix-up here . . .

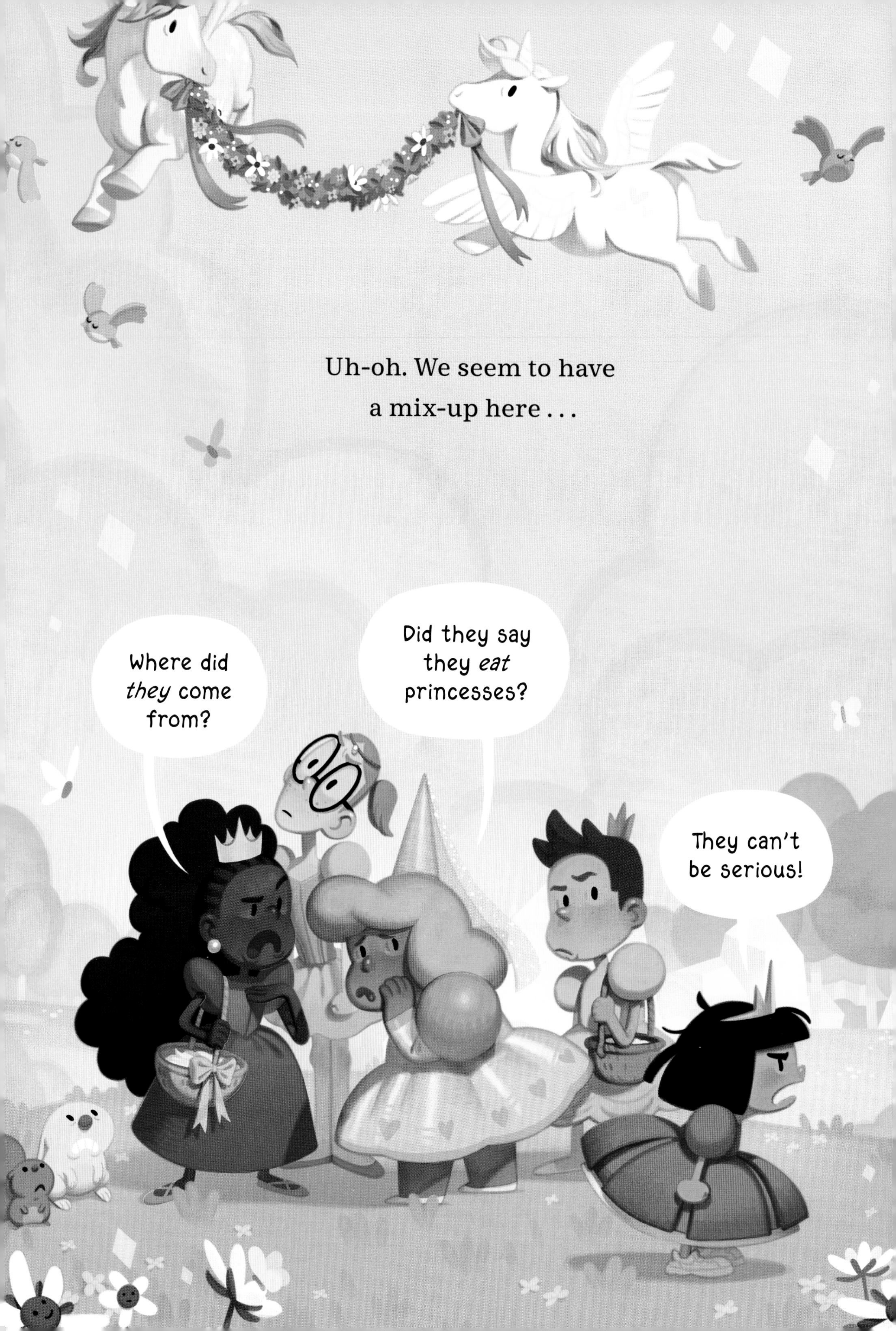

Whose book *is* this anyway?

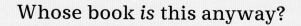

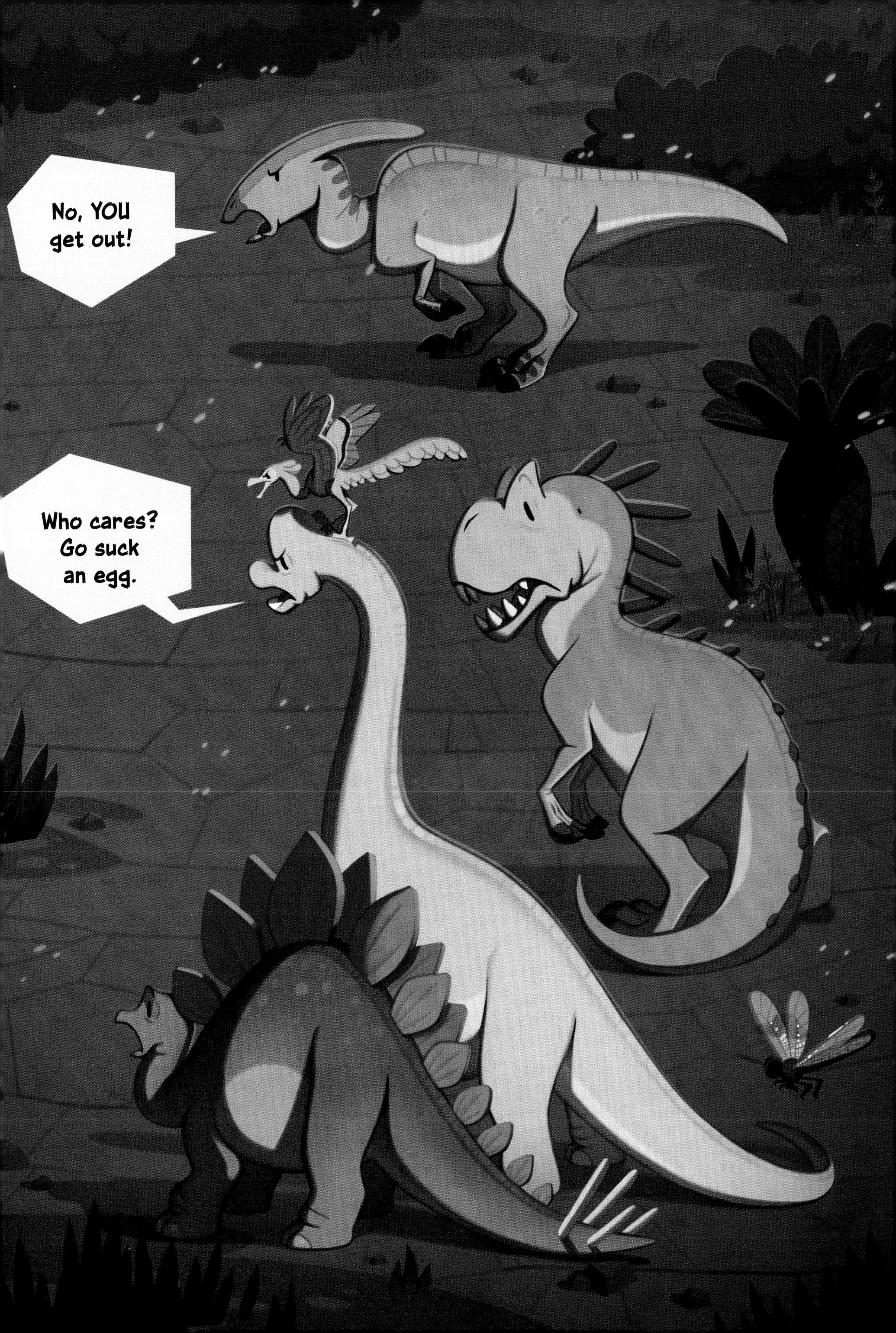
No, YOU get out!
Who cares? Go suck an egg.

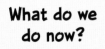

ROAARR

Maybe we should get Shirley.
SHIRLEY? Are you serious?
Do you think she'd come?
Let's DO it!

Hey . . .

Are you thinking what I'm thinking?

Yeah.
Hey . . .

I think so.
Are you
thinking . . . ?

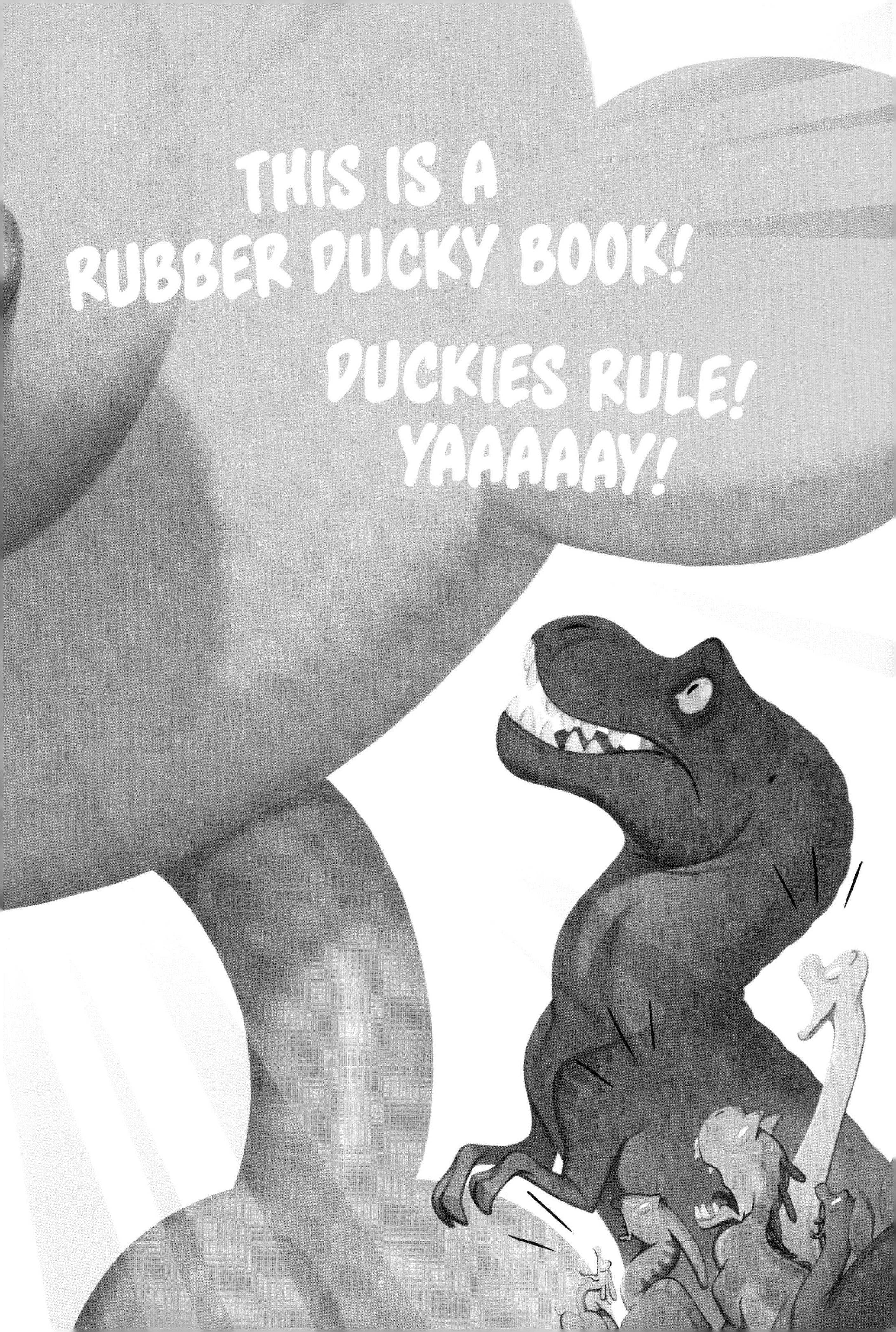
THIS IS A
RUBBER DUCKY BOOK!
DUCKIES RULE!
YAAAAAY!

A ducky? NO! That's ridiculous!
Who'd want to read a rubber ducky book?
Of all the nerve!

This wall is going to be soooo big.
Perfect! Keep those tiaras out!
Yeah! This is a WALL BOOK!

Well gosh! What's going on HERE?

This must be a princess
AND dinosaur book!

And look . . .
It's a dragon book too!
And a T-Rex book!
And a rubber ducky book!

So now we all know, right?

THIS IS A BOOK FOR . . .
# EVERYONE!